That is a Hat

**Story and Illustrations by
Betty Selakovich Casey**

THE ROADRUNNER PRESS
OKLAHOMA CITY, OKLAHOMA

For Max

Text and illustration copyright © 2014 Betty Selakovich Casey
Published by The RoadRunner Press
All rights reserved
Catalog-in-Publication Data is on file at OCLC and SkyRiver and viewable at www.WorldCat.org
ISBN: 978-1-937054-37-3
LCCN: 2014957123

Printed in December 2014 in the United States of America
by Bang Printing, Brainerd, Minnesota

First Edition December 2014

10 9 8 7 6 5 4 3 2 1

What is that?

Is that a tumbling tumbleweed?

That is not a tumbling tumbleweed.

I know what that is.

That is a . . .

. . . nest for my eggs.

Silly scissortail! That is not a nest for your eggs.

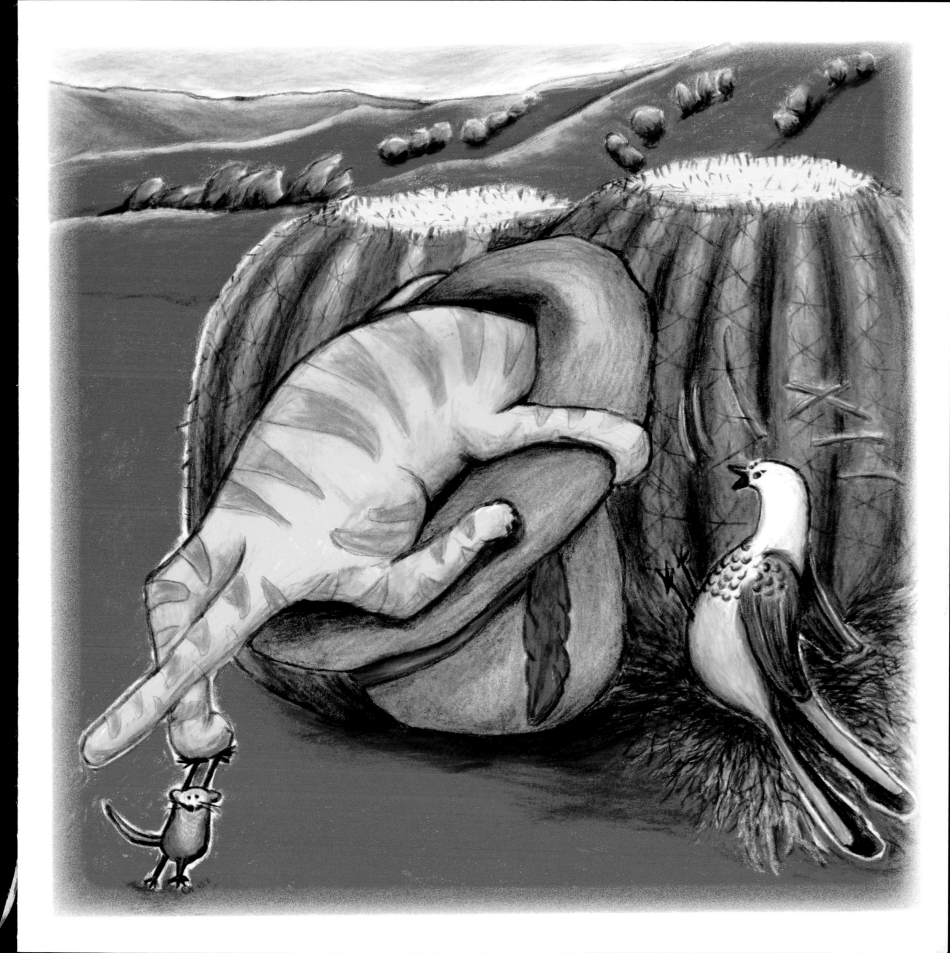

And it surely is not a tumbling tumbleweed.

I know what that is.

That is a . . .

. . . bed for my nap.

Silly cat! That is not a bed for a nap.

That is not a nest for eggs.

That is not a tumbling tumbleweed.

I know what that is.

That is a . . .

. . . toy to toss in the air.

Silly dog! That is not
a toy to toss in the air.

That is not a bed for a nap.

That is not a nest for eggs.

That is not a tumbling tumbleweed.

I know what that is.

That is a . . .

. . . den for my pups.

Silly coyote! That is not a den for pups!

That is not a toy to toss in the air.

That is not a bed for a nap.

That is not a nest for eggs.

That is not a tumbling tumbleweed.

I know what that is.

That is a . . .

. . . basket for my lettuce.

Silly jackrabbit! That is not a basket for lettuce.

That is not a den for pups.

That is not a toy to toss in the air.

That is not a bed for a nap.

That is not a nest for eggs.

That is not a tumbling tumbleweed.

I know what that is.

That is a . . .

Hat!

A hat!

What is a hat?

A hat is a tasty snack!

The End